YOUNG CAM JANSEN
and the
Ice Skate Mystery

by David A. Adler
illustrated by Susanna Natti

PUFFIN BOOKS

To Renée,
with love,
happy Silver!

PUFFIN BOOKS
Published by the Penguin Group
Penguin Putnam Books for Young Readers, 345 Hudson Street, New York, New York 10014, U.S.A.
Penguin Books Ltd, 80 Strand, London WC2R ORL, England
Penguin Books Australia Ltd, Ringwood, Victoria, Australia
Penguin Books Canada Ltd, 10 Alcorn Avenue, Toronto, Ontario, Canada M4V 3B2
Penguin Books (N.Z.) Ltd, 182-190 Wairau Road, Auckland 10, New Zealand

Penguin Books Ltd, Registered Offices: Harmondsworth, Middlesex, England

First published in the United States of America by Viking,
a member of Penguin Putnam Inc., 1998
Published by Puffin Books, a member of Penguin Putnam Books for Young Readers, 2000

17 19 20 18 16

THE LIBRARY OF CONGRESS HAS CATALOGED THE VIKING EDITION AS FOLLOWS:
Adler, David A.
Young Cam Jansen and the ice skate mystery / by David A. Adler ;
illustrated by Susanna Natti.
p. cm. — (A Viking easy-to-read)
Summary: When her friend Eric loses the key to their locker at the ice skating rink,
Cam uses her photographic memory to solve the mystery.
ISBN 0-670-87791-3
[1. Ice skating—Fiction. 2. Mystery and detective stories.] I. Natti, Susanna, ill. II. Title. III. Series.
PZ7.A2615Yon 1998 [Fic]—dc21 97-40256 CIP AC

Puffin Easy-to-Read ISBN 0-14-130012-4
Puffin® and Easy-to-Read® are registered trademarks of Penguin Putnam Inc.

Printed in the United States of America
Set in Bookman

Reading Level 2.0

CONTENTS

Cam Jansen has an amazing memory. Do you?

Look at this picture.
Blink your eyes and say *"Click"*
Then turn to the last page of the book.

1. LET'S SKATE

"I can't get my foot in,"

Eric Shelton said.

"Just push,"

his friend Cam Jansen told him.

"Ice skates should be snug."

Eric held onto the sides of the skate.

He pushed hard.

"It's in," he said.

He put on the other skate.

Then he tied them both.

Eric stood up.

"I feel so tall," he told Cam.

Cam stood.

She was wearing skates, too.

She was as tall as Eric.

Mr. Shelton, Eric's father,

was also wearing ice skates.

Cam, Eric, and Mr. Shelton

took their shoes off the bench.

"We have to put these in lockers," Cam said.

"I saw a sign when we came in."

Cam closed her eyes and said, "click."

"DO NOT LEAVE ITEMS ON BENCHES.

RENT A LOCKER.

LOCKERS 25 CENTS."

Mr. Shelton looked at the sign.

Mr. Shelton told Cam,

"That's just what it says."

7

Eric told his father,

"You know Cam has an amazing memory."

Cam opened her eyes.

"My memory is like a camera," Cam said.

"I have a picture in my head

of everything I have seen."

Cam says click is the sound her camera makes.

Cam's real name is Jennifer.

But because of her amazing memory

people started calling her "the Camera."

Then "the Camera" became just "Cam."

Mr. Shelton gave Eric a quarter.

Cam and Eric put the shoes in a big locker.

Eric put in the quarter.

He closed the locker door.

He turned the key and took it out.

Mr. Shelton said, "Let me hold the key."

Eric was next to Cam.

"I'm not a baby," Eric said.

"I won't lose it."

He put the key in a jacket pocket.

"Let's skate," he said.

2. CRASH!

Cam, Eric, and Mr. Shelton went onto the ice.

They held hands and skated together.

"Faster!" Eric said.

Cam and Mr. Shelton skated faster.

"Faster! Faster!" Eric said.

"I can't go any faster," his father said.

Eric skated ahead.

He skated around a group of children.

He went between a boy and girl.

A man and woman were holding hands.

Eric skated under their hands.

There was a large group of skaters ahead.

They were all holding hands.

Eric skated quickly around them.

He skated into the rail.

Crash!

Eric fell onto the ice.

Cam, Mr. Shelton, and a man in a green jacket
rushed to Eric.

"Are you hurt?" Mr. Shelton asked.

Eric looked up at his father.

Eric slowly shook his head.

"You were going too fast,"

Mr. Shelton told him.

"No," Eric said. "It was the rail.

It was going too slow."

"That's not funny," Mr. Shelton said.

"You must be more careful," said

the man in the green jacket.

He worked at the rink.

Mr. Shelton helped Eric up.

"I'll skate with you," Cam told Eric.

"Go slowly."

Cam and Eric skated together.

They went around the rink a few times.

Then the voice from the loudspeaker said,

"This session will end in three minutes.

Please return to the locker room."

Cam and Eric skated to the exit.

They were ready to get off the ice.

Eric reached into his pocket.

"Oh no!" Eric said. "The key is gone!"

3. LET'S GO! LET'S GO!

"Check your pocket," Cam said.

"Maybe there is a hole in it."

Eric reached into his pocket.

He turned it inside out.

"There is no hole," he said, "and no key."

Cam said, "Maybe you lost it

when you crashed into the rail."

"Maybe," Eric said.

He looked around the rink.

"But I don't know where I fell," he said.

Cam closed her eyes and said, "click."

She looked at the picture she had in her head.

"I know where you fell," Cam said.

Her eyes were still closed.

"Where the letters M L are painted on the rail."

Cam opened her eyes.

She and Eric skated slowly around the rink.

They found M L painted on the rail.

They did not find the key.

"Let's go! Let's go!"

the man in the green jacket said.

"I lost my key " Eric told him.

"You may take a quick look

before you go inside,"

the man said.

"I'll make an announcement."

4. CLICK! CLICK!

Cam and Eric skated around the rink.

They found a red mitten and a blue scarf.

They did not find the key.

They went into the locker room.

Soon they heard the announcement:

"A red mitten, a blue scarf, and a key

have been lost.

21

"Please return anything you found

to the office."

Cam and Eric returned the mitten and scarf.

They waited at the office.

A boy came for the mitten.

A woman came for the scarf.

But no one returned the key.

Mr. Shelton saw Cam and Eric.

"There you are," he said.

"Let's get our shoes from the locker.

We can get pizza on the way home."

Eric looked at Cam.

Then he looked at his father and said,

"Not yet, Dad. I'm thirsty.

Please, can I get a cup of hot chocolate?"

"Later," Mr. Shelton said,

"after we get our shoes."

"Please, Dad, may I have it now?"

Mr. Shelton smiled and said, "Yes."

Then he asked Cam,

"Do you want some hot chocolate, too?"

"No, thank you," Cam said.

Eric and his father went to the snack bar.

Cam sat on the bench.

She closed her eyes and said, "click."

She looked at a picture in her head.

She was trying to find the lost key.

Cam said, "click" again.

Click.

Click.

Click.

5. COME ON, DAD

Cam looked at the pictures

she had in her head.

She saw Eric take the key from the locker.

She saw Eric say he was not a baby.

She saw him put the key in his jacket pocket.

Cam said, "click" again.

Then she opened her eyes.

26

She put her hands in her pockets.

"Eric! Eric!" she called.

Eric hurried to Cam.

"Sit next to me," Cam said.

Eric sat on the bench next to Cam.

"No," Cam told him.

"Sit on my other side."

Eric moved to Cam's other side.

Cam said, "Now reach into your pocket."

Eric reached in.

"It's empty," he said.

"Reach in again," Cam said.

Eric reached into his pocket again.

"It's still empty," he said.

"Reach in again," Cam said.

Eric reached in and said, "Oh!"

He took out a key.

"How did this get into my pocket?"

"It wasn't in *your* pocket,"

Cam said. "It was in mine.

We were next to each other before, too.

You thought you put the key in your pocket.

You really put it in mine."

Eric used the key to open the locker.

He took out the shoes and called,

"Come on, Dad.

Let's put on our shoes."

He gave his father the key.

"You were right," Mr. Shelton said.

"You are not a baby."

"Of course I'm not a baby," Eric said.

"I can skate.

I can ride a bicycle.

And I can read."

Eric smiled.

"And I can eat pizza.

Let's go!"

31

Do you remember the picture in the front of the book?

Can you answer these questions?

1. Is Eric smiling?

2. What color is Eric's jacket?

3. Where are Cam's ear muffs?

4. What color are Cam's pants?

5. Is there anyone in the locker room?

Now read

Young Cam Jansen and the Ice Skate Mystery.

See if you can solve the mystery.

1. Yes 2. Green 3. On the bench 4. Blue 5. Yes